Pepi's Bell

by Shelagh Williamson
illustrated by Patricia Coombs

THE L. W. SINGER COMPANY, INC.

A Subsidiary of Random House

NEW YORK • BRANDON, MISS. • DALLAS • DES PLAINES, ILL. • MENLO PARK, CALIF.

Copyright © 1969 by Shelagh Williamson
All rights reserved under International and Pan-American Copyright Conventions
169.1   Manufactured in the United States of America   1A027
Library of Congress Catalog Card Number: 68-54983

In the land of Mexico
lived a little burro.
His name was Pepi.

Pepi was a happy little burro
except for one thing.
He had to wear a bell.
Everywhere he went, the bell rang.
Cling-clang! Cling-clang!

Pepi belonged to a boy named Pedro.
One night after work, Pedro had put
the bell around Pepi's neck.

"Now, Pepi," said Pedro,
"you can't hide from me.
I can find you when it is time
for work.
I can hear your bell."

Pepi did not like to work.
Pepi did not like the bell.
He ran into the big brown barn.

"I don't want to carry baskets
of corn to market," yawned Pepi.
"I want to sleep."

He lay down in the hay.
Cling-clang! Cling-clang!
went the bell.

"Cluck-cluck!" said the chickens.
"We work. We lay eggs."

"Baa-baa!" said the sheep.
"We work. We give wool."

"Ruff-ruff!" said the dog.
"I do my work.
I watch the sheep."

"Moo-moo!" said the cow.
"I do my work.
I give milk."

"Well, I don't like to work!"
said Pepi.

He stood up.
Cling-clang! went the bell.

"Oh, how can I get this bell off?"
cried Pepi.

He shook his head up and down.
Cling-clang! went the bell.
He shook his head back and forth.
Cling-clang! went the bell.

He put his neck down between
his front legs and rubbed and rubbed.
The bell went Cling-clang!
Cling-clang!

A little mouse watched Pepi
from the door of his mouse house
under the haystack.

"I feel sorry for Pepi,"
said the mouse.
"I would not like to carry
big baskets of corn to market.

I would want to hide, too.
I will help Pepi."

At last, Pepi lay down
and fell asleep.

The little mouse crept out
from under the haystack.

He began to chew on the rope
around Pepi's neck.

All at once—Clang!
The bell fell to the ground.
The mouse jumped back.

"Oh!" said all the animals.

Pepi woke up.
He looked down and saw the bell
in the hay.
He shook his head.
The bell did not ring.
He jumped for joy.

Just then Pedro called,
"Pepi! Pepi!
Come, Pepi! Time for work!"

Pepi ran out the back door
of the big brown barn.
He ran past the field of corn.

The other burros were waiting
to go to work.
"Where are you going, Pepi?"
they called to him.

"Good-bye! Good-bye!" cried Pepi.
"I will not carry baskets of corn
to market.
I will run away."

Pepi ran on and on.
He could not see the big brown barn.
He could not hear Pedro calling.

The sun was high in the sky
when Pepi stopped running.
"Now I can sleep all day long,"
he yawned.

Pepi was tired.
He lay down in the shade of a
cactus tree and fell fast asleep.

The sun moved across the sky.
It went down in the west.

The moon came up.
The stars came out.
A little owl hooted.

All at once, Pepi was wide awake
and very hungry.

He thought about the sweet corn
and hay Pedro would give him for supper.

Pepi was very cold.

He thought about his warm bed
in the big brown barn.

Pepi started to go home.
He could not find the field
of corn.
He could not find the big brown barn.
He did not know which way to go.

"Oh," he cried, "I am lost!
Oh, maybe my big brown barn
is just over there.
Maybe if I hurry, I'll be
in time for supper."

But just then—SNAP!
Something sharp caught his foot.

"Ouch!" Pepi cried.
He fell down.
His foot hurt.
He tried to move, but something
held his foot fast.
He tried to get up,
but the THING hurt more.

Pepi bent down and sniffed
at the THING.

"Who are you?" he cried.

The THING did not answer.

Poor Pepi did not know what
to do.
He was afraid.
He was alone.
His foot hurt.

"Hee-haw! Hee-haw!" he cried,
but no one answered.

Pepi licked his hurt foot.
One tear ran down his nose
and fell on the THING.
Clink!
Then, another tear — Clink!
Then, another — Clink!

"Oh, my!" Pepi cried,
"I want Pedro.
I want my bell.
If only I had my bell,
Pedro would find me!"

Just then, he thought he heard
a noise.
He lifted one ear and listened.
It sounded like his bell.

"Hee-haw! Hee-haw!" Pepi cried.

There was no answer.
Then he heard it again.
Cling-clang! Cling-clang!
It sounded far away.

Pepi tried to stand up.
He lifted both ears
and listened hard.
    Cling-clang! Cling-clang!

"It's my bell!" cried Pepi.
"It's Pedro!
It's Pedro with my bell!"

And it WAS Pedro.

Pedro ran to Pepi and put his arms
around the little burro.

"Oh, Pepi, I'm so glad I found you!"
he cried.

Then he saw the THING
on Pepi's foot.

"Why, Pepi," he cried,
"there's a trap on your foot!"

Pedro bent down and opened
the trap.

It fell to the ground.

Pepi rubbed Pedro with his nose,
just the way he always did.

Then he held out his neck
for the bell.

Pedro put the bell around
Pepi's neck, and they went back
to the big brown barn.
Cling-clang! Cling-clang!
went the bell.

"Oh, my bell sounds good!"
thought Pepi.

"Pepi's back! Pepi's back!"
cried all the animals.

Then they all had supper and went
to sleep in the big, warm, brown barn.